GIFT OF A NOBLE SPIRIT

(Ghost Story)

Pulak Kumar Chakraborti

BlueRose ONE .com
Stories Matter
New Delhi • London

BLUEROSE PUBLISHERS
India | U.K.

For permissions requests or inquiries regarding this publication, please contact:

BLUEROSE PUBLISHERS
www.BlueRoseONE.com
info@bluerosepublishers.com
+91 8882 898 898
+4407342408967

ISBN: 978-93-5989-352-5

First Edition: December 2023

GIFT OF A NOBLE SPIRIT

(Ghost Story)

Pulak Kumar Chakraborti

Others from the Author

1. ABHIJATTYA EBANG EAK EAKNAYAK

(Aristocracy and a Dictator)

A book in Bengali Published

2. PARK STREET THEKE PHERE DEKHA

(A look back from Park Street)

A book in Bengali To be Published

3. KINTU BHUT ACHE

(Collection of ghost stories)

Written in Bengali To be Published

4. GALPO O RACHANA SAMAGRA

(Collection of stories & other works)

In Bengali To be Published

Note : Due to Covid 19 publication schedule had to be rescheduled for early next year with a hope that things will be normal then.

In Loving memory

Of my

Father

Mother

And

Didi(Grand Mother)

They are with me

My Thanks

My sincere thanks to my Publishers Booksclinic Publishing and their employees of all divisions who co-operated in all possible ways.

Without their best efforts and co-operation the job could not be completed. It is important to mention that my Daughter in Law Rashmi did entire proof reading and edit job on the computer, without that I could not manage easily, thanks for her untiring efforts.

From The Author

My first book published in 2019 was about aristocrats and a dictator-Adolf Hitler. My next book is about Park Street and Mr. Jit Paul who gave Park Street the fame of business hub, prestigious commercial area. Mr. Surrendra Paul and Paul family were fully active to make it happen.

The Book was scheduled to be published and released but due to unprecedented COVID 19 crisis, the matter has been rescheduled for book release in Kolkata Book Fair 2021. Hopefully things will improve by then.

A friend in the world of book publication suggested me to write a Ghost Story in English which will have distinguished ghost characters. I am writing the stories of good ghosts which surely do exist in their world.

I would consider myself privileged in the event the kind readers like my ghost stories.

Forewords

We all have some of knowledge about ghosts, primary source being various stories heard and read. It is anticipated that ghosts do exit, they are good natured, bad and wicked. There is another type of ghost who are now shadow of what they were when alive.

This needs clarification. Some rich people have different life style. Babus, Landlords and other riches lived in their world. A high place of their creation. They were generous. The ghost here in this story wanted their hidden family treasure go to a family member and in the process of doing so the generous ghost made many rich including Satya.

I shall consider myself fortunate provided my kind readers find it of their liking.

Acknowledgement

We had free access to the palatial residence of a landlord not far from our house. Outer house had a Darbar hall with high ceiling and rows of tall round pillars, we had no business in that hall. Our destination used to be inner parts of the house to be entered through a ten yard (appox) long, dark and low height narrow tunnel. We had to crawl through the tunnel. I remember, was always scared of snakes in that moist dark tunnel. There was main gate, of course which led through the outer hall.

In this story I had in my mind that particular house.

As a very young boy I did not understand that the period I am talking about was the last stage of the crash of the land lord family.

For the sake of their right to privacy and the respect and honour I had towards the last senior member of that Land Lord family with almost nothing but the last senior member had mastered the knowledge and wisdom to talk about Rabindranath Tagore to Wordsworth, Shelly, Keats, Byron, Madhusudan Dutt, Milton and then the political leaders and education in Oxford, Harvard, Presidency, Calcutta University and many other subjects when we met. He was in the real sense a man of wisdom and education.

The Author

The Author Mr Pulak Kumar Chakraborti was educated in Kolkata, studied in commerce stream and then business management & administration.

He started his career in a commercial organisation having business interest in manufacturing cotton textiles items, export , trading and air conditioning & refrigeration.

His next place of service was with a large industrial house. He served with large and very large industrial houses mention must be made about Apeejay Surrendra Group, a famous and very large industrial house having diversified large industries. He served the organisation as Director for many years and retired from the services from this group.

My mother Mrs Namita Chakraborti, my wife Rashmi Chakraborti and our daughter Aarohi Chakraborti & me wish a grand success of this book.

Sandeep Chakraborti

Contents

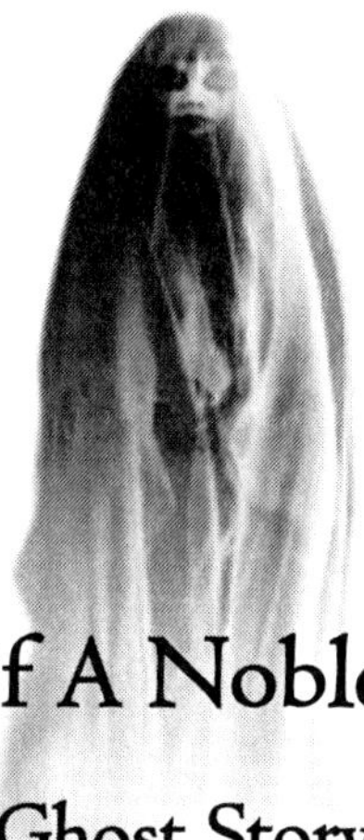

Gift Of A Noble Spirit

(Ghost Story)

Chapter one

It was the night of Christmas eve, 24th day of December 1984, a little before the midnight, Satya Mukherjee was travelling by a long-distance train and now the train has reached at Burdwan Junction Station, He needed to descend here from the train bound for Howrah Station, the end of the journey. Like many, this junction station was the terminal for him, others may be visitors or have some kind of business to do in their old town, traditionally the palace territory - a domain under the sovereignty of the then his highness the king of Burdwan. The palace witnessed the presence of great personalities, amongst them notables are Pandit Iswar Chandra Vidyasagar and the great Poet Michael Madhusudan Dutt. The great kings were known to be not only wealthy, but also for contribution towards the wellbeing of the society and education. They can be described in magniloquent words, but Satya himself now is in terra incognita place and needed desperately a way to reach his destination, not really a part of palace but an abundant mansion of landlord family,

The mansion is situated after the Punjabi Dhaba on high way from the main road one can see the once majestic mansion now in ruins except for a few living creatures still living in that mansion to take care of only almighty God knows what that could be.

He was made to know the presence of a quarrelsome lady, wife of the care taker to be precise. At this hour of night neither he can go there for shelter nor can think of any suitable alternative for his stay in this chilly night. First thing first-to look for a place for his night stay. He knows, there are hotels near the station. He decided to have a talk with the station master and started walking towards his office, with a knock he stood at the door frame of the room and upon asking his business at this hour of night, Satya showed his 1st class air-conditioned passenger's ticket.

The elderly station master has an inspecting look over the passenger who has just now established his bonafidee with the presentation of his first class AC ticket, indicated an empty chair for the passenger to sit and asked how he may help him. Satya, in reply told about the mansion he needed to visit and was about to say if the station having proper arrangement of stay for passengers which usually are available in big railway stations. The station master, upon hearing the first part of his question narrowed his eyes and tried to keep his feelings inside him, not to reflect on his face, yet his quench less quest questioned him if Satya was any kind of expert in exorcism?

Why do you ask such a question, Sir ? Then Satya told that he has other business associated with property and finance. He quickly added, Sir, I'm looking for the railway retiring room for my stay which I'm sure, you have.

Beyond any doubt, Yes, we have.

In that case, Sir, I would like to book my accommodation for 3 days. Can I have the breakfast facilities?

You can, replied the station master. While paying the money for retiring room, he made a special request for fresh bed linens and was a bit hesitant to ask for some food at this hour of the night. But on Christmas eve night, it was not a problem. Night was young and food of his choice was available.

By the end of the whole episode an under current of a kind flowed between them. During the waiting period of making the room ready for Satya, station master made a cautious approach to Satya, a polite question: if I may ask you what brings you to that remote and God forsaken mansion? Real reason please, you can choose not to reply.

Chapter Two

Satya found it as God gifted opportunity for information and help, information for the Project he has undertaken. With a little expression of shy, he ventured to formally introduce himself by saying I'm Satya Mukherjee, a resident of Calcutta, by profession a small time writer. My publishers literally is on my throat for a Ghost Story. It's easy to write a ghost Story, you know, story of "Bhut", anyone can write, but the kind of spirit my publishers likes, is a bit difficult kind, more difficult is the communication with that kind of rich, aristocrat spirit, could be considered with reference to qualities and character of noble spirit. Satya confessed that with the information he got, has every reason to believe that aristocrat spirits exits, even to this day, in that mansion and having interaction with those noble characters, he would be able to write a first hand account of ghosts.

He will stay in that mansion to know and note the life style, their attitude towards the common people and why are they living a life of ghosts.

Station master, after some thoughtful moments calmly made an observation-look here Satya Babu, myself Brajen Sharma living in this area and know the locals well. Burdwan is a big town, yet the people have not forgotten the old values and as a result the dead have carried along with their mind, not touchable and indestructible, the old values they have when alive, like the nobles, landlords and riches used to practice. During their life time they did many good deeds and lot of us have heard about the cruelty. But as the people say Roy Bahadur Chowdhury was good man.

By the way, do you have legal back ground? I mean knowledge about law ? asked the station master in a tone that reflects importance of the matter,

No, Mr. Sen, I'm not a lawyer, but know laws of contract and matters concerning property, replied Satya.

That might help, especially in the property matters, one of the ancestors of Chowdhury family fought a long battle and that ultimately was referred to the English court of law in Britain. Lord High chancellor of England delivered the divine order in favour of Ray Bahadur Chowdhury, friend of Britons in India.

Just an information, may be of some help, said Station Master.

Chapter Three

Satya went to the retiring room, unpacked few clothes and essentials for the night and the day ahead. He slept well. In the morning he left for Chowdhury Mansion, better to say, the ruins, by a rented car arranged with the help of Station Master. The car stopped at the grand gate, once that was and Satya went inside the mansion to meet any one of the living creatures, now in charge to take care of what is left.

He confronted a man who fitted as care taker, wanted to know the purpose of visit of an unknown man, an outsider.

He introduced himself as Satya Mukherjee from Calcutta, a writer on various subjects. His present mission is, with the help of this man standing before him to have a meeting with Late Great Land Lord Roy Bahadur Pratap Chandra Chowdhury for writing past history of this great family along with, of course, the man who now stands before him.

Cautious as he should be on duty of land lord, not visible now, but at his will may appear anywhere in this mansion. He replied that he is Jadu Das, living here with his family and gets paid every month from the estate office, now in Calcutta. He fathomed the man from Calcutta, supposed to be a story writer without bag and baggage, not even pen and paper, bluntly expressed his observation.

Satya showed Jadu his Railway ticket and told about his stay at Railway retiring room. Happy with the answer, he told him that he may allow the new comer to stay at night in one room, may even arrange a bed and food at a cost and without any responsibility, what so ever. Satya agreed and Jadu wanted a letter of declaration from Satya before boarding.

Satya agreed and gave specified assurance of his stay in this mansion; he left for the station to collect his luggage and paid advance money to keep the room. Arrangement for car parking to be done, though the driver, a local resident, did not agree for night stay.

Jadu shall take care of the car. In the event of any unwelcome situation the car can be of help for quick retreat to the safety of driver's home.

Satya had finished his dinner. Small part of this mansion has electricity connections, rest remains engulfed in total darkness. Satya was looking through the window and all he could see is black and black, no other colour. The solid black is beautiful, has a fearing feature yet inspired him for some unearthly experience. His chain of thoughts was interrupted with the knock on his door. He made the door ajar with an expectation of some one new instead Jadu indicated a dark portion of the mansion and said, the great Zaminder Roy Bahadur is now present in, once glorious dining hall, take this road. When you sense the presence of someone, switch on the electricity light, be sure, after taking the permission from his highness. We address as "HUZZUR", though you don't see him.

Chapter Four

As instructed Satya armed with a double cell torch light, pen and paper advanced steadily and ended his unknown journey before a door supposed to be the entrance of the glorious dining room of the by gone era.

He stood motionless, expectant of some miracle, heard a commanding voice-come on in. He stepped in and asked for Huzzur' permissions if he can switch on the electricity light. Upon getting the permission he switched on and saw the room with a big Victorian dining table of mahogany wood, curved lion's paw legs, couple of chairs, all not-in-so-bad condition appeared before his vision and not a soul present there.

He was standing near the table and heard the order: lay the table.

This order appeared to be perplexing to Satya. This did not escape the attention of not visible land lord. He thought that the man must be a surf, have come to his court for a favour. A voice from the un-seen enquired -What do you pray? At this, Satya got a chance to request the land lord, still not visible, that he is a small time writer and has been requested by his publishers to write a first-hand account of interview with an aristocrat like your esteemed self Roy Bahadur Pratap Chandra Choudhury.

So, in short you are an author. My family is known to support and pay due respect to the learned people made efforts to spread education. Before I do anything for you, have to pass certain tests, you Pass-ok, you fail , I shall lash you mercilessly and then there will be a small twist, half of a circle to make your chest as your back and back will be your facade.

Now let us have our food. I shall occupy the chair at the head of the table and you will sit on a right hand side chair. Put the plates, cutleries and napkins. Fill the glasses with water. You will act now as butler, hope you understand this terminology! It means-the person who is the head of man - servants and takes care, of drinks, Plates etc. In the absence of serving people, you serve me, then have your food, an honour for you.

Adjoining area, Satya thought to be kitchen which in reality was the butlery of this mansion and was all empty. "Huzzur" ordered to serve food. If he fails this test, Station Master cautioned earlier what his fate would be and he heard moments ago he may become a member of spirit society with reverse foot and head put on his shoulder in opposite direction from existing one. At this time most unexpectedly someone placed a sabre, a crooked sword at one side of table in the butlery and then steaming hot food items were being laid on the table. Although a novice about serving food to aristocrats, he first served "Huzzur" whom be cannot see, soup in a bowl, soup spoon, salt and paper. He noticed the movements of spoon and stood spell bound. With a sudden slap he came back to the world of reality and heard the order- main course and then dessert.

He received mild order- help yourself and he did. "Huzzur" declared that he will be back soon. With unexpected speed all the utensil and left over food vanished and Satya's bad luck started with a solid kick that threw him against the wall. He was on his four to rise, a hard slap accompanied with a pull of his hair against the force of gravity then pushed again to follow the law of gravity. He felt intense pain. Suddenly all vanished, heard the heavy thud of boot approaching towards the dining hall. Satya saw the time at his wrist watch. It was past 2 at night.

Chapter Five

Satya could feel the presence of spirit near him. He cannot see him. He so far has experienced nothing horrifying from the ghosts expect the extremely painful physical torture by low class ghosts. Those ghosts must had been once servants and kitchen staff.

The Rajas, land lords and riches are the members of aristocracy. They liked distinguished, grand stylish life and after death their souls carry the human qualities that had and live in another world out of human sight yet near enough to their kingdom, palace or the place they lived in their life time. Satya has to gather information and knowledge from the ghost about the present state of their life. With a respectful tone in his voice, he said -" Huzzur", during this night may we discuss certain points about the life after the soul leaves the living body. Reply came from an authoritative spirit yet possessing earthly dominating habit.

We now possess the quality of inner sight of a living creature and that I read your mind, the moment I saw you. You are a poor writer of some stories, not worth of being called literature. I have decided to help you in a way I like, like I helped the poor, needy and honest people. Now tell me your expertise in the field of law. I'm now telling you something which is totally confidential, must be limited between two of us. Do you agree?

Agreed-Satya promised.

Before I left my kings body about 80 (Eighty) years ago at the old age of 65 years leaving my wife, son and a daughter who had been married and was happily settled in her life. After my departure some bad human elements which include of my relatives too deprived my wife and son from their right to some of the properties I had and they were forced to live in Calcutta. They lead a good life there. This property where we are now is in the possession of my grandson, my legal heir. My wife had followed me long ago. My son is no longer alive. Jadu takes care of this palace, now in ruins. My ancestors had built up an interrogation room infamous for its use and character. It is still there in very bad condition. It has till this date the door for entry, and none have ever come out alive. Except very few none entered the room and came out.

My great ancestors had the brain and expertise to build a vault hidden from the eyes of the people and stored Gold coins, Gold Bars, Silvers, money and other valuables including a diamond that used to glitter on the gold crown which my great grandfather used to wear on special occasions like puja, family festival, parties thrown in the honour of important British rulers. I had naturally inherited the wealth and the crown. All in the safety vault of the torture room, couple of yards under the ground. You shall meet me in my other mansion where I shall discuss matters of importance and if all are well, shall instruct you about your next move. Be sure to keep your mouth shut.

Your next destination- Rajbandh. Take the car which you hired to night. He is a good man but never beyond doubt. Reasonable safety and pre-caution are needed. Secrecy is the keyword. You will find Choudhury mansion in Rajbandh on the right-hand side of the main road. Be there by II O'clock at night of tomorrow.

A sound of air as if a vaccum filled was and "Huzzur" was gone. In fact he was never physically present. His spirit, voice and a sort of feeling of some one's presence he could feel. Had he not been aware, he may not have sensed the spirit except the beating and pain.

He had no desire to stay. Drive himself to the station where he is booked for 3 days stay in retiring room, with a roar the brute force of the Ambassador engine jerked forward and soon Satya was in comfort of railway retiring room.

Chapter Six

Satya is early riser, but adventure of last night that lasted quite late resulting his sleeping even when sun was couple of yards up in the sky from the horizon. He made himself ready to go downstairs for breakfast. he sent some one, sort of bell boy, to find out if Station Master is free to meet him.

He is free to meet you- the man conveyed after his return. Satya went to the Station Master's room, two breakfast were served. Satya narrated the whole happenings without leaving a colon or semi – colon.

Like him, the Station Master was puzzled to the fact that the Land Lord did not appear in person enabling him to see. Anyway, that was the decision of the spirit of Land Lord.

Satya still felt the pain of last night's beating by a gang of ghost. Tonight, he is scheduled to go to Rajbandh and apprehend a higher degree of assault. He told the Station Master about this feeling and asked for his advice on a particular precaution if he should take.

He was asked to explain.

Satya was frank to narrate what his sixth sense is warning him for assault tonight. He has a plan to give the ghosts a run for their own safety.

He plans to carry with him to night at the mansion-

a)Iron rod - handy.

b)A cylinder of Dry-Nitrogen fitted with copper tube and hand shutoff valve. This will allow him to release high pressure dry nitrogen gas that may or may not hit the bad spirits.

c)Side by side he can release the valve of ABC Dry Powder Fire Extinguisher, the contents of which shall make the ghost visible. alternatively fire extinguishing foam may make them white.

Friendly Station Master, as he is now approves of his defence strategy and referred to a big refrigeration and Air conditioning company. He made a phone call informing that soon Mr. Satya Mukherjee would be visiting them and added that he would very much appreciate if Satya Mukherjee's requirements are met with for which he will pay.

He himself with another man and fire power, it can be a deadly defence. The works engineer made a small change in the list of items and suggested the following items:

A cylinder of Feron - 22 refrigerant, if released with full force will freeze them.

Fire Extinguishers as he wanted.

The works manager added a portable cylinder filled with F-22 refrigerant, Satya Babu will carry in his Sling bag ready to release the gas with a twist on valve. There must be one five cell torch with a sling.

Since he was the referred man of Station Master, faced no problem. He loaded the materials in his rented Ambassador, touched station to inform Mr. Brajen Sen the S.M. and headed for Rajbandh, ETA - 4.30 p.m., maximum 5 p.m. before the winter dark engulfs the entire area.

He reached the Rajbandh mansion in day light, parked his car just in front of main gate. Both wide and high pillars were standing with the massive colonial style iron gate with high boundary walls with signs of plaster that once covered the bricks. Satya rattled the lock on the gate and sound of which had reached the caretaker, opened the gate wide and invited Satya in and stood in anticipation to hear from this Babu about his business. On hearing Satya Babu's version, he introduced himself as caretaker of this mansion and requested to call him by his name Madhab Das, younger brother of Jadu Das. The trio unloaded the cylinders and other materials excepting those meant to be with him ready for use at emergency. By the time they finished the preparatory work, sun was about to go down. The western horizon was all in flame, red all over. This is known as dusk, time for the grazing cattle to be back home. As they walk fast on the dusty road, every friction of hoops with dust, the atmosphere gets dusty and probably for this reason this time is termed as GODHULI.

Chapter Seven

Satya for some reason is not exactly feeling at ease in this mansion. condition of mind shall change at dark midnight in the company of a good spirit. Expecting the presence of bad spirits and harm cannot be ignored and he has taken precaution to fight it out with the unknown and unseen enemies, if this could be anticipated so early. He informed care taker Madhab Das that he will be back before midnight, till then he must take care of the materials kept in dining Hall. Satisfied with the arrangements, he left the place with a firm resolution to come back before midnight, The night will be solid black and hollow sense will envelope this part of universe.

It is commonly said, Satya was thinking idly, that when there is no hope, it is referred to as " the future is black". But black is welcome in another sense to the world of others who we call ghosts, spirits called in this part of the world "Bhut" and the females are "pretni" . There is another section of "Holy" ghosts, known as "Brahma Daittya" or Brahman good spirits, clad in white clothes, lives on the Bel tree, Like lower sections of ghosts, these upper class are not bare footed. They wear the traditional wooden sandals used by the upper caste, the sages and holy men.

Which class of the spirit he may have to encounter with? One – the mighty Land lord on cordial terms with him, but even after death he will not consider him near equal but will be treated with the kind of respect the land lord gave when alive to people like Satya. Roy Bahadur, though a ghost now, have his own interest to un-earth the ancestral treasure to be handed over to his grandson (daughters excepted those days) who is living in Calcutta. He probably would be directed by Roy Bahadur to initiate a legal battle and fight it against those living creatures who have cheated Roy Bahadur's heirs. If ghosts, somehow come to know their plan of treasure recovery procedure, the evil ghosts will try to kill Satya for the final solution.

Satya is curious, have enough courage and scientific resources to combat the attack -to -come. His driver suggested a visit to a nearby industrial estate where his elder brother is employed as in-charge of maintenance of staff, officers' quarters, guest house and the Bungalow meant for the owners to live in when they come from Calcutta. The man here was not inquisitive, regarded Satya Babu as one client rented his brothers car like others do. They left the place, drove back to mansion, all in dark except a dim light on a post near the gate and rays of light that came out through the closed windows of dining hall. The driver parked the car, handed over the keys to Satya and left the place to live the night in some nearby place.

Chapter Eight

Satya armed with the materials carrying on his body started walking steadily without fear, he kept that faith in the mind. The court yard, before dining hall was also dark. He moved around during his first visit he noted that this mansion have two distinct divisions. The area where he is supposed to meet Roy Bahadur Chowdhury in the outer section of the mansion having exclusive hall for parties and entertainment for the landlords and their honoured guests. Britishers on special occasions like marriage, puja and important enough events that justifies the presence of English rulers and enhances the land lord's social standard and prestige. Court yard is surrounded with buildings and many rooms identified by their name, for example Nach Ghar (Dance Hall) , Pujor Dalan (Puja Hall), Baithak Khana (Formal Sitting Room for Outsider's) etc. Next part of the mansion has rooms for Ladies, Bed rooms, Kitchen, Stores etc with another court yard. The first court yard is big enough, to be a Badminton Court. Through a massive door that was once ornamental and witnessed many memorable entrances and tragic exits and quite a few dishonourable egresses inclusive of deaths, now and then a mute object in this household needed for the safety and security. This part of Bengal is chilly in winter season, around midnight in the open, the chill is biting, coldest breeze swept around accompanied with light rains.

Chirps of birds from nearby trees broke the deadly silence except the sound of sudden chilly mid-night air.

Owl and night flying birds cluttered with wings, Satya become stunned with the cluck, never heard at this time of night. The whole atmosphere magically turned into some kind of fear with awe and reverence and become anxious for the safety. He could understand that the stage has already been prepared. The characters of the drama, mainly the villains are waiting by the side of the wings of theatre stage. With complete disregard Satya steadily walked into the warmth of the dining room.

Chapter Nine

Sooner than his expectation, the authoritative voice of Roy Bahadur asked Satya to be seated, behind the totally obscure screen he remained. The land lord, announced the agenda of the night's meeting in the following order:

(a) Treasure

(b) Take same from the hidden place and

(c) Bring under the control of Roy Bahadur and then

(d) Satya to contact with the heirs i.e grandson of Roy Bahadur in Calcutta and finally.

(e) A fool proof plan to be made to hand over the ancestral treasure to him.

Roy Bahadur shall take care of Satya, from now onwards will be treated with due respect as the family's counsel. he will be, now being requested formally to act as the counsel including of course taking care of all things relating to law of the land.

With a nod of his head, Satya gestured his agreement. Meeting started. he heard the voice of Roy Bahadur Chowdhury that cautioned Satya to stay alert for unknown assault of any kind.

Satya could feel that someone has occupied the chair at the head of the table. The voice continued - You will never disclose, discuss, make known these secrets or divulge any of the secret information about treasure and its distribution to future owners.

At this point, with a loud thud someone invisible landed on the table and garbage started falling on the table and on Satya like showers. With an athlete fitness and ballet dancer's swift movement Satya from point-blank range sprayed the fire extinguishing foam on the unseen ghost whose position he correctly aimed for white foam spray and that made someone's large part of the body visible. Not wasting any opportunity Satya hitted the visible white part with the iron rod he had with him. Bone breaking cracking sound and with a hussh the ghost disappeared leaving parts of body bone in broken state. This unwanted encounter by the ghost clearly belonging to the opposite camp of Roy Bahadur sabotaged the meeting. For some reason the ghost did not make any attempt to harm bodily for which he was capable of, Satya did not dismiss this.

Satya declared the meeting adjourned for the night and be held during day time, the following day at eleven before noon. he asked un-seen Roy Bahadur if day light is a problem to him.

In reply, the land lord ghost explained that now they live in dark, but day-light cannot prevent their activities. it is true that lot of loss of energy and pain they have to withstand for appearance in day time. Considering the circumstances and his own urgency, he agrees. The meeting is fixed for transacting the business as per agenda already decided on the very next day at 11 a.m. Satya thanked Roy Bahadur and the meeting ended.

Note : cluck means the call of hen.

Chapter Ten

He came back to retiring room. He would need to meet the station master for some purpose and extension of booking of his room, if railway law permits.

Satya described the events of encounter with the bad ghosts. On first occasion they had tried to scare him and during the next meeting with the land lord those bad elements, if they could be termed as element, may not spare Satya, his existence may balance on the thin line of this world and the world beyond. The station master Mr. Brajen Sen, now much concerned about Satya's safety with the new bad players in the field, suggested to some lethal gas which can be harmful on ghosts.

After breakfast Satya rang up that Airconditioning and refrigeration workshop and made an appointment for discussion with their works manager and Chief Engineer.

Considering the gravity of the situation and life threating situation, they suggested about super cool Helium Gas, if released in full force in the direction of the evil ghost would surely cause harm. Satya wondered if that un-seen body is made of something on which very cool Helium Gas, Feron-22 can cause deadly pain and foam sprayed hits the ghost's body. Refrigerant and Helium shall form snow and white foam on white snow shall make the evil creature visible thus enabling Satya to give lethal hit. With the available materials with him, he would have to make his battle plan to win with hands down. he has made arrangement of transportation of Helium Gas cylinder to be stored with other cylinders.

Before midnight he started his journey towards the mansion and reached before the once grand main gate. Madhab Das was alert and quickly opened the gate and both of them started walking steadily towards the Dining Hall. Nothing happened except the gust of wind that passed and seemed to enter through the azar big door of the Dining Hall. Without giving importance to this Satya entered the hall and challenged the un-seen enemies – "Come on I'm here to settle any bloody score you have, I've none. Damn it, I don't know you."

His challenged went un-answered. Sooner than his expectation, Roy Bahadur Chowdhury appeared and his presence was loud and clear.

He was in no mood for small talk and pleasantries. He said in a grave voice, very commanding - this is my palace, all you see, I'm the owner. No one comes here without my permission. If any one dares, will be dealt with properly.

There came a quick reply with a shower of dirt that smelled foul, fell on the dining table and sound of thuds indicating appearance of un-seen bodies on the table right before him as the thud sound indicated. Satya wasted no time, with a twist he positioned the Helium Cylinder and released in full force which surely had hit the un-seen target and then sprayed the foam. Extremely cool Helium started forming ice which become visible and sprayed foam gave a distinct shape. As planned Satya was about to hit the object with the iron rod. Before he could act there came three rapid sound of gun fire and surely the bullets had hit the target. The effect was a sharp cry with tons of abuses and in reply Helium spray and foam were sprayed in wide radius that resulted in formation of snowy and white figure like object. Few more sounds of gun fire, the sounds were muffed as if the gun was made silent with the use of silencer. The evil ghosts started breaking things like chairs, China dinner sets etc. At this crucial moment Roy Bahadur made roaring command towards the evil ghosts - "Leave the mansion immediately, otherwise, without hesitation spray those gases and use fire power. If needed, Pour the Petrol and Ignite fire. Whatever we do, that is our business. You must have heard about hidden treasure. As ghosts neither you nor me have any use of them. On the contrary, my grandson, a living creature have much need of treasure and money. Leave at once." No one responded.

Satya looked around to see the source of gun-fire, but failed to see any. he felt a tap on his back and when looked back, to his dismay, saw an uniformed man with gun-in-hand. The uniform was of a private security guard. It was nor the time to speculate who and how this man came here.

At this moment Satya heard a woosh sound and rush of chilly wind indicated sort of exit. At this point the uniformed man with the gun made a move towards him and made a matter - of fact style statement - that station master Brajen Sen become worried about his safety from the cruel hands of evil ghosts and station master contacted one big factory of the locality. They had armed security guards. They keep licenced guns. The factory manager has sent him here to look after the security of Satya Babu and others. It was very good idea of his boss to send him here, otherwise by now Satya would have been a member of the ghost community and the security man ended his answer and observation of the episode.

Satya thanked him profusely and requested him to be there till the end of the meeting and asked Roy Bahadur for his consent to this arrangement. He also thanked the security person.

Chapter Eleven

The Meeting

The land lord though not in physical form, his soul in same form was all along there. He gave all clear signal which meant the evil ghosts have left and are scared of the lethal attack. Fire power in ordinary circumstances are useless, simply because the enemy could be air, gas or something capable of transforming themselves into shapes and sizes of their need.

His Highness the land lord announced that he would preside and with thanks he started.

1) The huge treasure accumulated over the decades are in the form of gold ornaments, gold coins and bars and silver in many forms could be weighed in kilograms. Besides these there are diamonds of many shapes and sizes. Roy Bahadur's great grandfather always used ornamental head gear; a big diamond secured with crafted gold crown that used to be fastened on the round head gear. There are many more precious stones. The entire treasure is like a king's wealth.

2) He continued that during the cover of night armed with the lethal gases and fire weapons, Satya would have to go into the underground vault where he would be met with very dangerous souls. They are by nature evil and dangerous.

Line Of Action

3) Satya is expected first to make those evil souls leave the underground vault. Once he is sure about his own safety he would have to drop down high-powered electrical bulbs of thousands of watts. Then with the help on secure stair like wide ladder he would go down with protective masks against possible poisonous gases and bring the treasure up.

4) The land lord further declared that the entire arrangement would cost lot of money and Satya is not expected to bear the burden. Roy Bahadur told Satya to go to his bed room of this mansion.

5) According to the direction given by Roy Bahadur, Satya went upstairs, the stairs though is not clean but in reasonably good condition. The big room to the south, facing a terrace was the bed room he could see with the use of torch light. The door of the big room was shut. He pushed the door open and waited for further instruction he is supposed to receive from the land lord. The land lord now directed Satya to look for a box in the corner of the room. He found one small wooden box, opened and found it empty. There are many compartments, quite a few are broken.

There is bottom section of this box. On the inner side of the lid he could read the name of the manufacturer "Lazarus" a famous company of olden days. In the bottom section of the box he found a bunch of keys, all rusted. The familiar voice instructed him to take out one particular key. Job done, Satya waited for further instructions. He was asked to go down.

6) Now, down in the hall Satya was told that his next job would be to go to the other mansions near the Punjabi Dhaba where he went on the first day, caretaker Jadu will be there. He should ask for the direction of "Underground Chamber". In the middle of the room, he would easily locate a trap door that

could be opened with the key in his possession, lift the door, use a stair Jadu will provide, make arrangement of enough light to be put down through the hole with the help of rope. Petromax should be ideal, suggested Roy Bahadur Pratap Chandra Choudhury. He cautioned Satya to be careful about poisonous gas. He must take help of modern scientific system to suck out the gas. After doing all this he is expected to go down with Jadu and bring the entire treasure up.

7) From nowhere a velvet bag landed on the table. The voice instructed Satya to open the bag. Satya opened the bag and found many gold coins, may be one hundred. Roy Bahadur Choudhury told him that these gold coins are known as Mughal Emperor Akbar era Gold Mohor, rare and very costly. Satya should encash these to cover the expenses of the treasure rescue operation leaving a good surplus amount.

8) Once cash-in-hand it would be Satya's duty to do the job. Once done, Satya must follow the instructions he is going to receive now. He should consider these as orders. He received following instructions:

a) Rupees Fifty thousand to be paid to Jadu in cash. Same to Madhab.

b) One fourth or divide the Treasure into four equal parts, Satya is authorised by Roy Bahadur Pratap Chandra Choudhury to take one part for himself. His share will be worth of King's wealth. Remaining portions, the three parts he would deliver to Roy Bahadur's grandson Anish Chandra Choudhury living at Ballygaunge place house. He should secretly meet him, hand over the treasure and explain to him that all have been done according to my order. There ends your duty and you live rich happily.

The spirit of land lord was now gone.

Chapter Twelve

Next morning Satya met station master Brajen Sen, by now a trusted friend and told him the entire story. Station Master read between the lines and told, Satya, you have done the entire job and must remain faithful and only then you can live rich. Never, ever, think of any dishonesty.

Now you have no option but to kill one living animal, simple way would be to put one or two small pig, young hog in a cage and down that into the underground room, wait for some time and then lift the cage up. If they are alive, you are lucky, still repeat this process three or four times in different corners of the chamber. If those are found dead, that will mean presence of poisonous gas and that has to be sucked out before one enters there. Try the cage method tonight.

By noon, Satya transported all the cylinders of lethal gases and informed the caretaker Jadu to be available at mid night. Jadu came alone with a long rope and the cage, a hog inside. With the help of Jadu he cleaned the floor, un-locked the trap door, swung it open, saw the bottom with the torch light, found nothing dangerous. He put the cage down into the room with the help of rope, waited for few minutes, pulled up the cage and to his surprise found the hog alive. He repeated the process in four corners and the result was same. Satya thought hard and finally decided to go down into the underground room after lighting two petromax and one torch light of five cell Satya had and a three cell in Jadu's hand. Jadu kept handy few hurricane lanterns. Jadu was wise enough to keep jute sacks and twine. A big coil of thick rope was lying in the floor.

Chapter Thirteen

Preparation to go down to underground chamber is complete. Satya had checked the ladder's strength and became sure that this will not break.

He tied securely one end of rope to his waist and the other end tied with a pillar. Instructed Jadu to keep sharp eye to the rope for signs of vibration of rope. If there be any vibration, he would pull him up.

He will wear the safety mask. Once all arrangements were done, he double checked everything, made sure he did not miss or overlooked or neglected any small detail. Satisfied with arrangements, he started to descend and landed into the well-lit cell. he located the treasure in a big secure box and opened with the key. He was told about this by Roy Bahadur Chowdhury. He found Gold Coins, Bars, Ornaments, Diamonds and the special big Diamond for head gear of the Land Lord. The treasure was heavy enough. Jute sack and twine was useful to haul the treasure up.

Once up in the room Satya became nervous about the danger from criminals who might be around. He took Jadu into confidence and wanted a place of safety for some time. The cylinders have to be kept over there for the night. With that in mind he paid rupees Fifty thousand to Jadu as directed by Roy Bahadur Chowdhury. Jadu did not expect this huge amount of money. Satya promised him further payment in near future as loyalty bonus. His brother Madhab will get the same amount.

The car was parked near the entrance, not far from here. Jadu suggested that since the car is there it's better to clear the place from all cylinders and other items. Tomorrow, either he would have to come with the treasure or keep it to some place and both the options are not very acceptable. He with the help of driver will load everything in the car in no time. During this discussion Satya was distracted a bit and suddenly his heart was about to go out of his mouth at sight of the treasure sack being lifted by un-seen hands up in the air. He, in a speed of striking cobra, released the valve of dry nitrogen aimed towards the sack and at the same time released Helium. These worked. The sack landed on the ground. Satya made no attempt to go near the sack, he could be hurt or get some injury from the unseen devil whom Jadu and Satya have to tackle and win in establishing his right of possession over the treasure.

Moments passed in deadly silence. Suddenly some giant got hold of the ladder and at that very moment Satya and Jadu both understood what may happen. Both took shelter under the massive dining table. The ladder like a hockey stick attempted to hit them. The factory manager who at the request of the Station Master had supplied all these cylinders, supplied a gas cutting set and nozzle in case any iron safe or iron Almirah needed to cut. Satya lighted the flame and increased the gas flow resulting a much bigger flame. He then put the flame on empty jute sack threw up in the air on the ladder. In no time the big jute sack produced a big fire on the ladder. The common belief is that the spirit cannot stand fire. Satya thought, if it is true then soon, he would see the result. Sooner than he imagined the ladder fell on the floor, wasting no time

Satya jumped up on the table and started cross cutting the flame in the air hoping to hit the evil spirit he cannot see. The result was good. A chilling cry and Hussh sound made them sure that the evil spirits have left the room. With the help of Jadu and driver each and every item was loaded in the car. Careful inspection made to be sure no clue left there to connect some body's presence expect the ash. Leave it there, we got to go. The driver started the car, engine roared and bolted out. Jadu was with them. He had shifted his family somewhere and would stay there tonight. The car brought him to station in the safety of railway retiring room with the jute sack. The driver will take the rest to the factory to return. Tomorrow, Satya thought he will settle all accounts. He kept the sack in the corner of the room by the side of head board of his bed and threw few old newspapers on the gunny sack and soon he slept.

Chapter Fourteen

The situation and condition both were averse to a good sleep, but he needed physical and mental rest, he has much to do on the following days.

Station Master knew about his night adventure and came early to station. Satya met him early in the morning, He securely locked his room and made sure housekeeping staff cannot enter with the help of master key. He had to request Station Master to make it sure because the treasure is there. He is about to tell everything to the Station Master soon.

He told Station master that his share, one fourth of the treasure, he wants to sale and needed help from the Station Master for the simple fact that he wishes to pay both Jadu and Madhab, the care taker brothers for all they have done. Further payment for car rental, driver with bonus. The workshop, to be paid in cash.

Satya begged to be pardoned for his next approach, should Brajen Babu found it offensive. He sincerely requested not to mind for what he is saying now. To sale his share of treasure he needs the help of Brajen Babu, in fact, he would totally depend on him. Brajen Babu has done a lot for him and without his help to combat the ghost would have been impossible and reach to the treasure. He would offer Brajen Babu a good amount in cash.

The Station Master agreed. He assured Satya that this is not anti-law or any sort of stealing. The Land Lord, now living in another world beyond the reach of human being, have given him the authority and provided with help and clue to reach the treasure and allowed twenty five percent to him that he now legally owns.

The station master will call quite a few big jewellers to his Railway Quarter Residence and dispose of in small lots. All to be finished in two days and by the end of day Satya must leave by road.

He made a master plan for his safe departure and safe journey right up to the residence of Land Lord Roy Bahadur's grandson Anish Chandra Chowdhury.

Satya would buy some good conditioned old furniture and household things. He will declare that he is leaving this town and going to Calcutta with the furniture. He will also travel in the same four-wheeler.

This is a perfect cover. Lot of Railway or other Government and Private sector people get transferred and he is one of them. By midday of the second day sale of treasure, purchase of furniture and loading in a small track were complete. Brajen Babu gave Satya an old Suitcase to stuff the money and clothes. With that in hand Satya said good bye and occupied a front seat of the mini truck. The journey started and he hoped that this would end by night fall or later depending upon the traffic situation.

Chapter Fifteen

The game plan was chalked out keeping the priority in mind that his first place of visit will be the house at Ballygaunge Place to hand over the treasure. He does not want to be there more than an hour. Having done that he would have to come to his Paik Para residence in north Calcutta and un-load the old furniture which would fit in his flat. He made purchases keeping the need in mind.

He reached Ballygaunge Place by early evening and announced his arrival and wished to meet Babu Anish Chandra Chowdhury.

The house was a big one of yesteryears' Land Lord with Victorian furniture, Precious Paintings, Old Carpet in Sitting room, Mahogany wood made Sofa Set tables those need polishing and better care. Curtains are not in a good shape. During the observation a tall gentleman appeared and asked for Satya's business. he had the style of old era riches.

Satya replied that he has come to meet him as per the direction of Land Lord Roy Bahadur Pratap Chandra Chowdhury and talk to Babu Anish Chandra Chowdhury relating to a very important financial matters of their estate.

Satya, in all seriousness said that since he does not know or cannot be sure about the identity, he requested Anish Babu to show some identity papers; without that he cannot complete the big financial business. Please, I'm in a hurry, Satya put that as request.

Without a word Anish left the room and came back with two cards issued by the Government department. Satya compared with the photograph of card with the man in front of him. Satisfied with his identity Satya stated the story, all chilling parts and ended with his arrival at Ballygaunge Place house with the treasure still in the jute sack.

Anish closed the windows, bolted the doors and put the entire treasure on the table. Satya especially showed Anish the great diamond that Anish's ancestors wore on the head gear, now shall cost a fortune. There are "Mohar" of the Emperor Akbar era, gold coins, gold bars, Precious Stones etc.

Anish could not believe his eyes, nor could believe that anyone could be so honest to hand over this King's treasure.

Satya told Anish to take care of this vast fortune and said in no un-certain terms that received a quarter part of the wealth as was decided by the land lord himself.

Anish was not at all worried about that portion Satya had got. He was thinking of safe keeping of the whole lot.

He was in deep thought. Satya wished him good luck and good bye and left the room after Anish carefully opened the door

Back in the mini truck, much before one hour, the truck run fast towards Paik Para. He climbed down unlocked the flat door, kept the suitcase and unloaded the furniture, got those fitted and placed in the rooms of his flat. He then paid the truck with generous extra and they happily left for their home town.

Between the four walls and ceiling of his small flat Satya always felt secure. In his locality, he is liked by almost everyone. People in general respected him. For the first time of his long stay in this flat, he felt lack of security for keeping that kind of cash in the house.

Satya is an honest man. This money he has earned in a hard way risking his life. Money earned with hard labour is legal money, but who will take his story of ghost giving money. Suddenly it appeared to him that Babu Anish Chandra should be able to help him. With this in mind he reached the Ballygaunge Place house of Anish next day. He was received cordially. He explained Anish his dilemma, his problem and sought his help in legalizing the money. He will pay the taxes.

Anish found out a way. He explained -Your share of Twenty five percent is from our family treasure and legally I'm the owner. You give me the money.

I don't have it with me.

Please go and bring back the money, then we discuss business- Anish told Satya.

Instantly Satya decided that he will take some chance. This is risky, Yes, he would take the risk. He came back to Ballygaunge Place house with the old suitcase containing cash.

Give the suitcase to me- Anish Babu asked.

Here you are-Suitcase changed hands.

Now the money is not yours, it is mine. You are a writer. I'm appointing you to write a story of our family, about my ancestors and for that you must visit our ancestral mansions, stay at night and write your true experiences. This is a risky job, you may end up dead. Yet I'm ready to take the chance under these conditions; Anish observed:

You will write the true story. Both of us will be the writers, written by me with your assistance. Do not worry, I shall add valuable inputs which you will never know, not possible to go that deep.

We will make an agreement stating all these clauses and other terms and conditions. I shall pay you in advance in cash an amount of money that equals to the money you got. By the sun down of fifteenth day from today. You will deliver the story to me.

On stamp paper agreement written, checked, xerox copy made from an outside shop, both of them signed witnessed by two persons, Anish arranged.

Anish now handed over the suitcase to Satya told that this is your remuneration paid in advance for writing the true story. Before the due date Satya did deliver the goods - the story.

Anish read the story and was happy.

He certified Satya as good writer. Satya told that he is an honest tax payer and will declare the income in his income Tax return.

Babu Anish Chandra is very active man. He decided to go to College Street to certain Publishers to publish the book. Initially the Publishers did not show much interest but Satya's name did work.

Financial terms and conditions are not relevant here and not really needed. What is needed are the other details, like-the book will be Hard Cover with Jacket. Anish's ancestral mansion will be coloured photographed for the cover; a professional will design it. There will be at least eight photographs of the various parts of mansion.

The book titled as
GIFT OF NOBLE ANCESTOR

Anish Chandra Chowdhury

Assisted with on the spot experience by

Satya Mukherjee

A known author

The book will be released soon.

THE END

Characters

1. Satya Mukherjee – An author who had the on the spot experience

2. Brajen Sen – Station Master, Burdwan Railway Junction Station

3. Late Roy Bahadur Pratap Chandra Choudhary – Landlord, decorated with hon'ble title – Roy Bahadur by British rulers for his services to the British Emperors in India.

4. Jadu Das & Madhab Das – Both are care takers of Choudhary Mansions

5. Babu Anish Chandra Choudhary – Grandson of Roy Bahadur

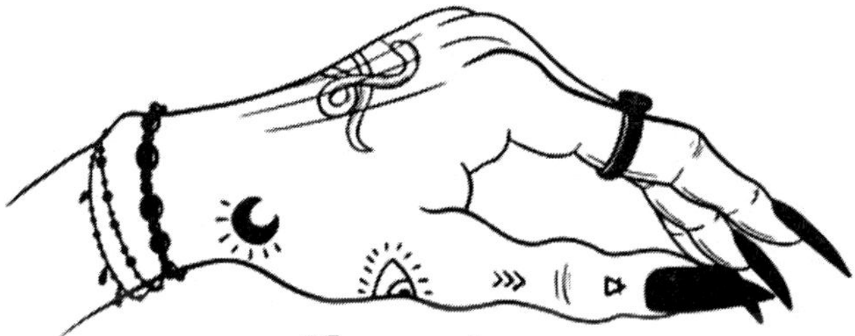

Exorcize

(Exorcism is widely practiced to drive away the evil spirit by magic words and by the strength of prayers)

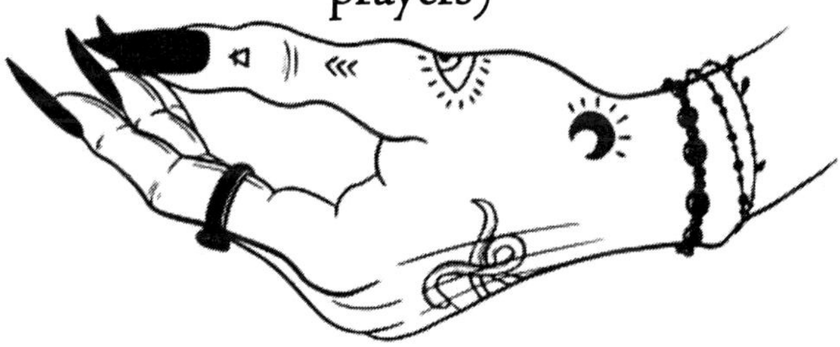

Chapter -I

My readers are kind and good; goodness is more infectious than wickedness. Thus, quite a few got infected and they read my books. I am a compulsive reader, read whatever I get, poetry, drama, novel, thrillers and even calendars. On a journey by British Rail I got a calendar, it was year-end, the desk calendar was for the next year, a beautiful calendar on wild life. Lion. Royal Bengal Tiger, Leopard were main players. The pictures described their characters, origin, habit and the sleek body, burning bright Royal Bengal Tiger, the king Lion – I kept reading.

All book lovers and readers have good collections of books, my assumption. It may or may not be correct but I have good collection of books. One may wonder how could I afford Shakespeare, Shelly, Keats, Milton and other big names of English literature. I leave this subject of collection including its way to the people who can understand

I am known as a good and compulsive reader, not many people have seen my collection of books bought from economy shops with signage – "pay one pound and take any two books", it is good and affordable. Mr. Malcolm Smith has a vast collection. I took from him, rather borrowed many books to read. What had happened actually? I forgot to return the books and Mr. Smith neglected to keep a record of books given to the borrowers. In course of time these books became my books.

I make frequent trips to those economy shops to add books to my collection. Very recently the two books I purchased, one of them was titled THE ENTITY, story of super natural forces, primarily torture on woman. When in London I stay at Metropole hotel near the Marble Arch and when in Birmingham I do like to maintain the same choice.

In general, the ghosts are wicked, they kill human being and cause pain and harm. They roam around at night – this is the usual belief but contrary to their night haunting characters, there are many ghosts who prefer the "days" for choosing their would-be victims. Ladies usually have soft mind and nature. The ghost can "possess" the lady, live on her to do the wicked things, yes, yes, that happened six decades ago. The place of occurrence was an Indian Tea Garden. Breaking news of that morning was – newlywed young girl "Bandana rendered powerless by a ghost, devastated girl raves …" Namdanga tea garden in Assam, was a quiet, nice and big tea garden. Mr. Hampton Fairweather, the garden manager rushed to the bungalow of the garden doctor whose just wed young wife is under the bad influence of a ghost, that's the news. As the tea estate manager reached, the atmosphere over there changed, he got all the attention. He was taken to "Bandana" who was sitting on the floor, clearly looking tired, un-tidy and querulous. This is her newly acquired skill by the time ghost got hold of her.

Mr. Fairweather was greeted with a volley of missiles in the form of abuses it was no lady-like behavior.

An exorcist is on the job, trying to drive away the evil spirit by means of torture. Materials needed to create a fire ball that would be thrown upon the victim. The expert assured that the fire will cause pain to the ghost, now thrown on the young girl.

The exorcist threw a fire ball on the face of the girl and demanded the evil spirit quit at once. The devil flatly denied. He would teach the girl manners and etiquette.

At this Mr. Fairweather lost his cool.

He roared – you wretched devil, a mean creature, what the hell you want to teach her ?

Sir, manners, please do not forget the British culture and modesty. You don't follow any of those in your colony. But this country earned the freedom.

This is pure rebuke, thought Mr. Fairweather and the evil spirit spoke a language of different league.

: Who are you? Garden Manager demand. I will iron out the corners and make the girl free, promised Mr. Fairweather. He gestured to the exorcist to stop for the time being.

He asked the ghost what was his problem.

: Do you remember your onetime dishonest assistant John Paul?

: He was here is this garden long time back.

: What this girl and your bloody modesty and etiquette have got to do with?

: You knew he was a killer, and you sacked him one fine morning.

John Paul killed one labour and the body could not be traced. Lot of people expected the labour will come back home.

The dead could not come back.

: Who are you talking about? Make this long story short. I do not have whole day for you, snapped the garden manager.

: The dead did not come then. The same person who was killed by John Paul is here to seek justice.

: Then the matter damn well should be between the two of us. Leave the innocent girl alone, thundered Mr. Fairweather.

: I agree, let's first sort out the issue concerning this indecent girl – the ghost declared.

: Proceed, said Mr. Fairweather.

Right at this point the exorcist called the husband of young girl and said – I understand, I had a mission to accomplish and that is to drive away this devil of a ghost out of this garden and to the other side of the hill. May I proceed gentlemen and Mr. Fairweather?

: Please go ahead, was the reply.

Exorcist : Why are you so bent upon to cause harm to this innocent housewife.

Voice of the girl : I live on this mango tree for all these years I can remember. Last night I was sitting on the guard rail of the balcony. The girl came out badly dressed, in complete disregard to my presence, an unknown man. She showed me dog defiance. I do not tolerate this. She has to pay for her folly.

Exorcist : How many lights were on?

Ghost : It was dark.

Exorcist : Very good point for you. You were sitting in dark balcony and your skin is black. You just melted with the black night. How on earth she would have seen you? Had it been with you, I am sure you would be sailing in the same boat. You are as old as hill. Your eye sight is weak. You do not wear spectacles. With this kind of eye sight how can you be sure about her dress? You anticipated. Whatever may be your position in the dark world of ghost, the verdict I pronounce will be effective from this day of August,1970.

Ghost : Why she came out not properly dressed ? I do not like exhibition.

Exorcist : She was going to washroom at midnight. Not a soul was there. Forget your century old logic. You must leave and leave now. Otherwise I'm going to burn this heap of red chilly

Give me the reply – say – yes.

You have to go away from this tree, and out of tea garden.

Ghost : No, I do not agree. May be, out of compassionate attitude, I would have pardoned her had my interest, most important, my living place and dwelling condition be considered. Treat my problem with compassion. All the trees in this tea estate are occupied.

Exorcist : Go you must. Trees on the south of the "Happy Nook" garden are free. You can go and live there. I assure your accommodation.

Ghost : I agree.

Exorcist : You have to prove. There is one big brass vessel full of water.

You lift that vessel with the bite of your teeth.

Show it to every one present here.

: Do it, I know you can do it.

The ghost inside the girl gave a bite, all present there saw the girl to give a bite and lift the vessel off the ground.

The stage was ready for the ghost to leave. The exorcist demanded a proof of his departure. He demanded that the ghost break a big branch of the tree as he departs.

Ghost : Agreed. I'm off from her body and soul. Let her promise to be decent in future.

I was very young then, was standing amongst the people gathered there. I still remember the perplexed look of the girl, she was astonished to see at least one hundred odd people standing there, a sage type of man clad in saffron colored clothes was sitting in front of her. She enquired what was happening there! Her husband moved forward. Their conversation was very serious and intense. This is extremely dangerous, whispered the young housewife. No one is safe now.

The saffron clad exorcist came forward and told the young lady not to worry about things that happen sometimes back. The ghost is leaving forever. He turned and spoke in the air –

: Now you leave this place and while living as a proof break a branch of the tree you lived on.

Now go, commanded the exorcist. Moments later a big branch of tree, as if someone unseen had axed and the branch fell on the ground.

That was the end of Assam story of ghost. Our entire family went to the tea garden to attend a marriage ceremony. It was sheer co-incidence that I happened to be there and could witness the super natural activities. From then on, I keep on looking for characters in my story.

Chapter -2

While I was writing the Assam episode, I went there, stayed for few minutes and now I am back at London Metropole. I travelled mentally; it is faster than any speed ever invented by human being. The speed of mind is so fast that it can take one around the world in matter of few seconds and that is how I travelled to Assam. Ghost can travel very fast. I have no knowledge of measuring their speed.

However, I am back to my 19th floor hotel room planning to go to the fair at Institute. This fair is basically organized by a council deals with the development of Arts and Crafts of Bengal.

This council through its efficient and big network are able to reach the remote villages where artisans work on various crafts like crafts of Brass, few metal mixed together i.e craft from the alloy, cane, bamboo etc. Amongst cotton textiles varieties are sarees, embroidered bed sheet, bed cover, table cloth, tea cozy cover, sofa covers – embroidered beautifully, eye catching colour combination and these items are available in cut work. Besides these there is one craft which is – layers of cloth put together, say six layers and are stitched together. The stitches could be hem, long stitch, chain stitch etc. Then designs are stitched – these are fine stitch for flower design, figures – anything. They are poor men's blanket.

Dedication and efforts of a lady in Calcutta brought a revolution in the world of "Kantha" by introducing better skill, materials, artworks etc, and the end result was astonishingly beautiful Kantha with high class stitching and design. Thanks to the lady for revival of this craft, which was not in very good shape. Kantha is not only used by financially weak people, but also it has made a place in the rich household.

This council operates from Calcutta and having its office there, Hon. general secretary of the council is Mrs. Ruby Pal Chowdhury. They are well known rich industrialist having interest in various industries.

London is now free from smog and pollution has reduced remarkably. Evenings and nights are clear. I started from Baker Street to go back to my hotel. A known face had side passed me, he travelled with me in the same compartment and got down ahead of me at Edgware Road and headed for exit. I had a plan to go to Marks and Spencer and then to Boots. Both the establishments are not far from London Metropole, a short walking distance.

I recognized the man who was walking ahead of me. This is the man who left the book in railway compartment. I took that book. I myself made the life threating mistake. I did not know then, and not even now.

Abruptly, the man stopped, and came face to face:

Can you please help me? This is heavy, carry it for me, will you? He took his head off his shoulder, head in his hand, offering me to hold. At this sight I saw all yellow in front of me, thousands of yellow flowers and probably I fainted.

Next, I found myself in a room, appeared to be a room of hospital or some sort of medical room.

On my request, they told me that friendly London police found me lying on the road just outside Edgware Road tube station, unconscious with no mark of injury on the body, no sign of any attack or a physical assault. Police searched my pocket and could find papers on me; those papers directed them towards Metropole as place of my stay. Police brought me here with two Paramedics and treated me in the hotel's treatment room. Now that I am well, Police left leaving one Para medic with me. I wanted to go to my room on 19th floor. The Paramedic consented; since he will be staying at night, I made a request to the medical man that he can stay in my room, a separate bed will be provided with. I conveyed my wish to hotel admin who promptly arranged an extra bed but declined to take extra charge which I offered.

In the morning I felt fine. Both of us had sumptuous English breakfast. Now settled on the room sofa, in the cool comfort of hotel room, the medical man wanted me to describe the whole thing in details, not leaving any incident, however, insignificant that might be. I narrated the story starting from British Rail journey, Edgware Road tube station and all that happened on the road.

The medical man asked me if I know any meaning of this super natural harrow. I agreed to tell him what I knew.

According to Hindu Mythology Goddess Kali appeared headless and her severed head drank her own blood came out like fountain from the neck. I cannot explain the inner meaning or the reason for such action because of my short coming about those religious facts. I did try my best to explain Goddess Kali to this medical man.

If the ghost try to play any trick or get me into danger, in that case the ghost should be allured to church where he could be rendered powerless. Father Keating would be of great help. I should try to take the ghost to central Pentecostal church or Adventist church where the holy men of the church would help me.

The medical man further added if I am not making any mistake, he requested you to hold his severed head and you fainted. Next time if this happens there's some advice for you. You carry a big draw string bag with you. In case of request to hold the head, take it, put into the bag, secure by drawing the string then run for your life to the nearest church or any busy place. Keep this fact in your head that the ghost is without head, therefore cannot afford to go to any place like a market where too many people are around. He thought of destroying the head of the ghost but dismissed the idea because that might lead to "killing" and get punishment. Better option would be to preserve the head and negotiate, discuss for something good. You are in a position to command, make him obey you. We will see what happens.

My mind became clear and strong to face anything that may come. Now, I decided to go to the fair. Amongst many items, King and Queen size bed cover without any joint having fine needle work all over is in good demand. A big departmental store was keen to have these bed covers. I actually invited them to the fair. They showed positive interest and then we negotiated, I gave offer letter, they accepted and as per terms have opened Letter of Credit, shipment by AIR. I knew the source of procurement of ready goods. Bed covers as per order have been collected in Calcutta and shipment made by AIR. Our shipping agent in London will clear the consignment by noon and arrange delivery to the buyer at their Oxford street departmental stores. By arrangement, buyer's representatives shall be there with our shipping and clearing agents. Upon delivery of goods at the store, they will call me to go there. I started to get ready.

Chapter -3

The telephone in my room buzzed, at the other end was our clearing agents. They informed that by 12 noon the consignment should reach the stores.

I told them that I shall be at the stores. I reached at the stores before 12 noon and saw one cartoon was ready for opening. After cutting the nylon straps and adhesive tapes, unwrapped the poly sheet that covered the polybag packed bed covers, ultimately came out the bed covers. It was satisfactory. In charge of that department told me that the packaging is too good for air shipment. We can cut down our cost here.

From Oxford street I started for Paddington, reached around one o' clock and had decided to finish lunch before going to fair. I headed for a restaurant where I had been before. It serves good food at affordable price.

I finished my lunch quickly, went to the cash counter to pay. The proprietress herself takes payment. I gave a five-pound note and pat came the reply – "on the house, free for you." Another customer who was just behind me was leaving without paying. The lady called him and asked for the payment. That customer, I must say was quick witted, promptly replied – "he is free" – indicated me and added – I thought I'm getting same privilege.

Come here mister, please pay. He is "on the house" because I like his face.

I was startled, saw a young lady sitting behind the counter.

I had tried to reason the young lady to take payment from me but her "no" became sweeter and sweeter.

I found out later that 'mother' sits at the cash counter but on this day, the daughter was there and because of her liking my face, declined to take payment.

On my previous visits I saw the lady at cash counter and she took payment. Today she was not there.

I became impulsive and thought of avoiding this place but on second thought dismissed the idea, planned for a visit to make the young lady understand the business and personal life should not be mixed together. I wanted to be there in this afternoon to resolve the issue.

Keeping this idea in mind I came to fair, went to meet the Director of this institute and found he is not there, took left lobby and was on my stride. On the floor of the lobby I saw a cuddled "Quilt", paid no attention, passed by and reached the fair hall. I saw a few were looking for a quilt that is missing.

I remembered the quilt on the lobby floor, told them what I saw.

Here, I cannot resist the temptation of quoting few lines from a poem of Rabindra Nath Tagore. A poor translation from Bengali to English by this author done in order to express what we all feel in such cases:

You will agree –
it has no wings? an object
either gets stolen or lost,
a cheater may cheat
or it stays – otherwise
what else, not known to me.

They reached to the cuddled quilt and surprisingly a lady was underneath the quilt, she protested as they were picking it up.

Why are you lying on the floor covered with quilt?

I am suffering from high fever, feeling cold and sick, she replied.

Immediately she was taken to the office, doctor was informed about high fever and a request was made to visit ASAP.

One of the organisers came to the office room, told the lady to remain seated covered with a shawl. She picked up one book from the table and asked – whose book is this?

My book, I kept there.

Where did you get such dirty book?

One passenger left the book, I took the book with his consent.

She held up the book with two fingers and asked if she can throw the book away.

I consented, she told me – never, ever take anything from a stranger. This dirty book may have germs and you have been infected.

I promised her that I shall sanitize myself just now and I did.

I did not know a deadly virus in the form of ghost have entered me.

A discreet enquiry done by me revealed that mother and the daughter duo are running this establishment while mother looks after the finance, and daughter is in the charge of administration. It is a nice family restaurant. Employees of nearby offices patronize this place, they are regulars. The daughter Miss Dorothy Lane has completed her graduation in Economics.

She must be a good student. Economics is tuff subject. She has got beauty and brain both. A blonde of medium height and with deep blue eyes has natural attraction. In the event of absence of her mother she takes the dual complete charge.

Chapter -4

At about four in the afternoon I entered the restaurant almost empty, she was behind the counter, our eyes met. I took a table opposite the glass counter. She can see me through the glass. I settled on the chair, glanced at the cash counter and saw a serving boy coming to my table. I ordered for tea and snacks.

Sir, would you please sit in our exclusive room meant for important persons, Miss Dorothy Lane would be delighted to join you?

With pleasure, I consented. I consider it as an honour, I added.

Please come – this way and he led to a room, well decorated, with a big window.

While I sat told the waiter – I'm comfortable.

After couple of minutes Miss Lane entered the room clad in a dress of lighter shade of new green and white combination.

I got up, shook hands, formally introduced myself and she did too.

We talked about the bright day, few words on weather. Discussed business, education and student life. She holds a degree in Economics, she must have been a brilliant student.

We talked about Oxford, an institution of more than seven hundred years.

She asked me if I live in England. I replied that I come to England four to five times a year. I told her in brief with an emphasis that her place is very conveniently situated for the people who come to the institute. It suits me for its proximity and good affordable food.

I did not forget to give a small but meaningful lecture about keeping friends and business separate.

Finance must be protected then managed and fresh wealth to be created. Most important is protection of money.

In reply the business lady replied that "on the house" is an important tool of business promotion and it rarely fails. On the contrary, with a wicked smile Dorothy said the gain is fast.

I understood what she meant.

The tea was "on the house", notwithstanding.

Chapter -5

The ghosts may have the ability of reading the mind of their target, single out the victim and they strike. This is the common feature of wicked ghosts. We have no way to know their nature unless they show.

The ghosts have expectation, not for themselves but for their near and dear ones. I think a small amendment to above statement is required. The ghosts expect no money, no wealth but they expect a kind of religious ritual to be performed for them in order to be released from present ghost life to a better life. After the ritual the soul will be free from present life.

They can move and act as they like. Maybe they have some limitation. The logic behind my such thinking is the ghost's behavior, I analyzed that and came to the conclusion – that he is trying to create a web of fear around me and then would ask me to do some job for him.

He is trying to push me back on the wall, I will have no place to move and be compelled to work for him.

Now my firm resolution is to be fearless, to remain calm, tactful and be with strength of mind.

My afternoon meeting with Dorothy was a very good one. In the course of discussion, I gave her a hint about my books already published. She may like my latest publication "CREATION OF WEALTH."

This does not tell you the ways and means of making money. She suddenly became respectful; wanted to know where this book and my other works may be available. I assured her that five books shall reach her. I shall bring it tomorrow round one o'clock.

I'm inviting you for lunch. I agreed and left the place, thanked her for everything she did including her valuable half of an hour for tea session.

I am back to craft fair for discussing the possibilities of quick procurement of king and queen size seamless white pure cotton bed cover with stitch work self and contrast. The product has good demand. Big chain stores could be our buyers. I'm working on this possibility. I was informed that good quantities of such bed covers could be supplied. This will be a good start. Compared to other bed covers, these hand embroidered self and contrast bed covers are quite costly. The customers are dedicated, they go for these bed covers. I'm idling with the idea of introducing other products of this variety. Items like tea tray cover, tea cozy cover, napkin, sofa head and hand rest would capture the market, my study of market indicates.

I stayed late in the craft fair. From Paddington took tube, reached Edgware Road. Not many passengers were there. Someone walking ahead of me towards the exit. I came up, was waiting for the signal to cross Edgware Road and head for London Metropole.

I saw a man coming towards me with long stride, stood in front of me face to face.

Unmistakably the same face of the train, the same man whose book I took, the same ghost requested me to carry his head.

I steadied myself, tried to think of melted steel flowing into my veins. I waited for him to talk on this lonely road.

He broke the silence, can we talk?

Not unless I have to, was my curt reply.

You will be willing to co-operate with me after you see what I shall show you soon.

Now have a look, the man started to grow taller and taller, I had to look skyward to see his face. It was done in matter of moments and he was back to normal. I was unflinching and stood firm.

The ghost thought his action has terrified me. He said with authority – Now you are compelled to dance to my tune and then you will be eager to work for both of us, am I clear?

In the meantime, give me the draw string bag you have, said the ghost.

How do you know I have such bag with me? I asked.

How do you know I'm a ghost? Not a magician of high caliber?

Now it is my turn to demoralize the ghost, to do so, I acted swiftly: look, you are not a big gun. You are a gun of short range, low caliber and small bore.

He looked perilous, ready to attack me, now turned himself into a tiger, only the face. I knew if I loose my courage to fight him, I may be a dead man.

I thundered – you wanted to know how I knew you are a ghost! No, I did not know then in the railway compartment. Father Andrew Keating of Adventist church detected your presence on me and applied his power and will force to reduce your ill-effect.

Do you understood, you thick headed but I must admit you are a good natured and well-wishing soul. The last two words of praise was my trap. The ghost has to submit, with this in mind I asked him to tell his identity and then what he needed? Maybe he wants to do something which he cannot do.

What if I don't reply? – the ghost was adamant.

Your waterloo – was my sarcastic remark

What? Asked the puzzled ghost.

Never mind, it means – you loose.

I started – if you come open with your identity, your need, my role, benefit if there be any, maybe I shall consider to discuss, I repeat may be, after I hear what you want.

Can we sit somewhere? The ghost asked.

Yes, let us go to any of the two churches I told you.

Why church? The ghost appeared uncomfortable.

That suits me. What is your problem?

At this, he explained – to enter a church or a religious place he has to do some cleansing of his body and soul.

Then do it – I ordered this time.

Chapter -6

He was meek now; said he would do the purification job while we walk to church. He added that he would not be comfortable there. But he said the need is mine, therefore I shall go to Adventist church.

Once settled on a bench, the ghost started – "I shall reply your questions:

I'm a Briton, was in India during the second world war, amassed huge wealth and kept it safely in my house on B.T. Road. My family had gone on "Home" leave. I was in India alone. Who can deny God's wish!!

A nasty road accident took my life and I do not know why I am a ghost with no fault of mine. The ghost stopped.

What do you want of me? You have not said you name yet, I said.

Ghosts have no name. It is not important here to know who I was.

It matters, tell me quickly.

He took no notice or ignored.

In those days walls of the house used to be thick. My B.T. Road bungalow have thirty inches thick walls. Those are load bearing walls. Hope you understand what is load bearing?

I nodded in affirmation.

The fact is – during the period my family had gone home , I constructed a partition wall between the dining room and outer space which had wooden folded decorative partition. I wanted a permanent one. I ordered to construct a thirty-inch-thick wall. Head mason Rehman told me partition wall can be ten inches thick.

No, I want a heavy rather grand looking wall.

Rehman very politely asked if he can say something? Talk between Englishman and a native used to be in different manner, not in the manner I described above. We were the rulers, treated general natives below the standard.

But I was different, from a different league, used to give the natives freedom, my subordinates were a happy lot. I was liked by them, I knew.

However, he placed the idea before me, an unique one, I must admit even today. His idea was to erect two five inches thick walls with a hollow space of twenty inches in the middle, with side covered will look thirty inches. Other side has existing wall and ceiling on top.

It might collapse – I expressed my doubt.

No, huzzur, it will be all right.

If you do not like ....

I interrupted – do as you suggested, but erect in the evening when I am in the house. I want to see it.

The masons erected the small six feet long wall complete with one side covered. It is looking like a thick wall.

They left and I started my job. The wall was wet then. I removed bricks one by one from the wall and through the hole had placed my treasure into the void area, placed the bricks again, did the masonry job as best as I could. Next morning plastering job was completed.

The B.T. Road house is in ruins. My son and daughter were very young then, son a toddler and daughter – new born. I told you about the accident. My wife was in England, was leaving in Manchester then.

You need to know our names.

I was Adam Scott

My wife is Dolores Scott

My daughter – Rebeca Ray, nee Scott.

My son – Philip Scott

My son-in-law Anil Ray and Rebeca were good friends and as the time passed, Rays and we knew that this relation is firm and in time, they will marry. My son Philip was doing well. He started looking after my business of imports of steel items which was in demand during the war. Lot of people became rich, you can say that was the result of war.

Post-independence, India needed more steel for many projects of the country. He made a fortune and had bought this Loudon street property. It's a big house, constructed two dwelling units into one. Philip lives in one part, big enough with six bed rooms, Rebeca's side is of equal size. She lives in her house in Auckland place but comes to Loudon street to meet Philip quite often. Now, you have got the full history of our family and geography as well.

Chapter -7

My B.T. Road Bungalow is a big property known as Scott House. It is the walled property just after the cigarette factory. You cannot miss it. It has a tennis court, lot of fruit bearing trees are there. The house is in ruins due to absence of maintenance. Forcefully occupied by two families, not known who are they. But they have local support, I feel.

Now, listen to the Modus operendi:

The house was owned by Dolores and me.

After my accidental death my wife had got the ownership changed and had recorded with the authorities. Now listen carefully.

: You have to go to Mrs. Dolores Scott and tell her everything I told you including the treasure.

: Make her know that I have given you the assignment of wealth recovery from my house.

: The house is in bad shape, unauthorized occupiers living in that house, it is trespass.

At this point I said –

: Mr. Scott, please take no load on your head about the present condition. Everything can be put under control. The unauthorized occupiers have to be dealt with: When they are satisfied with the compensation amount, they will vacate. This could be arranged through a lawyer without breaking any law. Go ahead Mr. Scott, let's finish it quickly.

: Mr. Scott started explaining that: Mrs. Dolores Scott will agree to give you lease right on the property for five (5) YEARS WITH LEASE RENT OF SAY Indian Rupees 2500.00 per month to be paid yearly, Rs.30,000.00 at the beginning of the lease.

Termination clause: 60 days' notice either side, after expiry of 2 years.

Most important thing we have not discussed yet. Your professional charges, I would like my son will pay you under this head for the services rendered by you. Today, the valuation may stand at about five million Indian Rupees, to be distributed equally amongst four persons including you.

What is your opinion?

I asked ghost specifically – Why did he go in such a complicated way? He could have told me straight away.

I also put another point – Where's the guarantee that I shall get my 25% after the treasure is recovered and handed over to your son? Why did you not tell your son to recover your hidden wealth?

The ghost replied – Mrs. Scott will give you the property on lease, details you know. You are protected. Discuss with your lawyer before you agree. He did not reply my question.

I thought it myself and gave a condition that may be considered. That is after expiry of lease period of 5 years your son Mr. Scott Jr. shall consider my offer to buy this property. Other terms and conditions shall remain unchanged.

The ghost assured that Mrs. Scott will take care of these points.

YOU WILL NEVER REGRET YOUR

DEALINGS WITH A GOOD GHOST.

As discussed with the ghost all were done exactly as planned.

Back to India, I took the professional help of Chartered Accountant to take care of accounts side, ensure payments whatever we have to pay.

A good tax consultant took care of everything.

Expenses: Paid by four in equal share.

TO READERS

Near the end of this ghost story, I request my readers to believe that good ghost play the role of good host.

You choose to deal with a good one, shall not regret a deal.

I got what I had to.

Author's note

A parcel of five books wrapped in gift paper, was handed over by me to Dorothy the next day. Over the lunch she saw all the books gifted to her by the author sitting with her, the books were signed by the author with best wishes and regards to her. This delighted her.

She became a good friend and we are in touch. We meet whenever I am in London and take the advantage of on the house.

During the second world war B.T. Road property was not costly. Now the price has increased many folds, yet Mr. Scott sold that to me at such a low price you would not dream of it.

It is good to have a good ghost as a friend.

THE END

Tamarind District

Pulak Kumar Chakraborti

Chapter -I

Haripada Mondal, a rich resident of Sundernagar had planted Tamarind trees by the four sides of his big pond. A dozen of trees, now have grown big, covering completely the four sides of the pond. Of all trees what made Haripada to plant Tamarind trees is any body's guess. May be, tamarind gives good return. You get a high price. He planted the trees without having any idea that ghosts, both male and female love to live on tamarind trees, reason not known to me.

It is believed that ladies like to eat tamarind with spices, sugar, chilly and salt mixed together and naturally like to live on tamarind trees. But what about male ghosts? Anyway, the ghost of that area wanted to live in their own state, ruled by them, their own law, own system of punishment and reward too. Thus, Tamarind district was formed. Mr. Bobby Lewis became the Prime Minister. It is important to give some description of newly formed ghost state and their P.M. too. Twelve tamarind trees, each tree with well spread branches measures about two thousand square feet and twelve trees would be admeasuring twenty four thousand square feet.

The ghosts of this block assembled together in one dark night under the leadership of Bobby Lewis. Bobby Lewis was a policeman posted in local police station. He was a good football player. After play, Lewis with others used to swim in the pond. Some times when the sun was up on the head, he would come and see the spark on the small waves created by breeze. It looked like thousands of diamonds sparked on the water.

Surely, he had a poetic mind. It is not known why Bobby Lewis came to swim at the dead of night at this pond and found floating in the pond next morning, long dead.

He became a ghost. As a police man and good football player he was quite popular and was in command. After death, his command was established over the ghosts of this area.

Twenty four thousand square feet of tamarind tree area was the office and residence of prime minister and other ministers, officers, and lady ghosts.

Something nasty in nature happened in the ghost kingdom. Ghost Mantu Das has abducted a young house wife who is now sitting on the ground in a haze, totally confused. How a ghost dared to abduct a living young lady. Most disturbing is the fact that some of the ghosts are supporting the action of abduction. The young house wife had a fight with her husband and in an angry state of mind she left home only to be abducted by ghost Mantu.

Bobby Lewis decided that entire government of ghost must be changed in such a way that he will be in total command of the state – the Tamarind District.

He called an emergency meeting and summoned four captains of ghost army, they are captains of North, South, East and West fronts. He demanded total support from each of them personally and the army, in return they will be rewarded.

The meeting started at midnight. Bobby Lewis, at the start of the meeting thanked all ghosts of this state for their discipline and moral.

But abduction of lady who is still alive can not be tolerated. Surprisingly a section of ghosts have taken the side of abductor. This is punishable offence.

Bobby placed the most important matter for the discussion and the resolution passed without any objection from any quarter.

He pro : Four captains of North, South, East and West promoted to the rank of Field Marshall from this moment.

: Ghost Atul, Moti and Dhiru promoted to take charge as General and to take charge immediately.

: Ghost Sudhir, we inform you that we are pleased with your public relation job. We, therefore appoint you as Minister-in-charge of Public Relation and allied affairs.

: The last but one, is to increase our Army for expansions of ghost empire from these twelve trees to more secure and comfortable places.

: Finally I want to change the name of our state from Tamarind Republic to Tamarind District.

: With this I declare myself as the ruler – Dictator of newly formed state and government to be formed before the end of night.

: Now I ask – anyone who want to oppose – raise your hand.

: No one objected. Resolutions passed unanimously.

There is no democracy instead a dictator shall rule them.

Ghosts are not ambitious. They do not like their present state of life they are living. Some one may not accept this statement, might ask, pray, tell me when and which little bird whispered in your ears such a not-so-believable words. None told me but many firmly believe that certain rituals done at "GAYA" would free them from the life of ghost and they look forward to the ritual to make end of a life of spirit. Therefore, my statement above mentioned is based on this circumstantial evidence.

Any way, there is more important matter in hand than the argument. The new ruler ordered to bring the abductor ghost before him – all powerful ruler.

The young ghost, a fresh vegetable from the garden prepared to take the punishment, came forward.

You will be tried now, announced Field Marshall East. You will be given fair chance to support your act and justify yourself without any assistance from lawyers.

The abductor under trial said in a loud and clear voice - I plead guilty, conditionally.

What is your condition? Asked the field marshall. My guilt though grave in nature, can be rectified without much difficulty. The lady can be sent back home. When she is back home and living under no-stress, my guilt ends there, that is my condition.

The dictator replied – accepted subject to the successful implementation of rehabilitation.

He also added : Who will take the lady home ? How will that be done ?

We shall take the lady to her home. At night she came out of home quite agitated. She was taken from there.

Taken? Is she any vegetable? Rebuked the supreme ruler.

The ghosts have no eyes, they have skull and hollow eye sockets. The alleged guilty had lowered his head in order to look down on the earth, can not meet the eyes (if they have at all) of the ruler. Bobby Lewis dismissed him for the time being and called Madhuri, the new arrival.

Chapter -2

The ladies of ghost state usually live a separate life. Madhuri arrived before the all-powerful ruler and stood. She was waiting for the question. Lewis came to the point straight:

The young house wife sitting on the ground is in a haze. To be sent back to her family without causing any harm and you will have to see that she will not be in trouble in her house. How will you do that?

I can not go there as a ghost. I shall go there in disguise of a rich lady. My story would be that I rescued her from ditch, in her confused state of mind, took her to a place of safety. After nursing she could tell this address and I am personally here to reach her home. Lewis liked that idea but was doubtful in his mind. Madhuri showed intelligence again, she read the supreme leader' mind

She again assured him that things will go well when in disguise of a upper class lady wearing glittering ornaments and style will do the job. That family will be grateful, they will submit before wealth and personality. Do I have the permission to make a move, my leader?

You do not have to address me as my leader. I hate it. I'm a big follower of socialistic pattern of Democracy. Don't ask now why I have preferred to be a dictator. Madhuri, you carry on.

With the flash of a lighting from the sky Madhuri re-appeared.

Madhuri was standing before Bobby Lewis, wearing gold, diamond and pearl jewellery set and said with a smile "I was on my way to attend an invitation, found the lady in distress…".

Perfect, please finish the job and be back as soon as possible. We have important matters to discuss.

She left with the lady for her house. She is a bit better now.

How did you reach here? Lost on the way ? Madhuri asked her. The lady nodded.

Let me take you to your husband and your family. Where do you live? enquired Madhuri.

Beside the playground, she replied.

It's not far off, let us walk, can you?

Yes, I shall, she replied, and then the duo reached and found the family members on the courtyard. As soon as they saw her, all ran towards her and got a shock, a lady of very rich family with her.

Madhuri maintained her high status and told that she found her in distress etc.

Every one of that house gratefully thanked her, offered her a seat and was in dilemma how to entertain this lady from a high and rich family.

Job done, Madhuri wasted no time, advised the members of the house to take care of her and left.

Madhuri returned at ghost speed and found an extra ordinary emergency meeting has been called by the ruler of the Tamarind District to discuss and implement two very important matters.

Madhuri arrived. The ghosts were looking at her in awe. She remained in her make-up. Bobby Lewis started to conduct the meeting.

First point of the agenda I propose to end the dictatorship and be back to a democratic state, name remains the same : TAMARIND DISTRICT.

: I shall be the Prime Minister, as I was.

: All in favour say "Yes."

Prolonged "Yes" was heard. All in favour.

Second item of the agenda : Madhuri shall become my deputy in the ministry with independent charge of education, culture and development.

Those who want to oppose say "No"

Pin drop silence.

It means yes, said P.M.

There was a cheer-Y-e-s.….

The ghost state – Tamarind District functioning well under the leadership of Lewis and Madhuri as deputy.

They, as a rule, never harm any human being.

THE END